My Weirder-est School #11

Mrs. Stoker Is a Joker!

Dan Gutman

Pictures by
Jim Paillot

HARPER
An Imprint of HarperCollinsPublishers

To Andrei Thomsen

My Weirder-est School #11: Mrs. Stoker Is a Joker!
Text copyright © 2022 by Dan Gutman
Illustrations copyright © 2022 by Jim Paillot

Library of Congress Control Number: 2022931764
ISBN 978-0-06-291085-1 (pbk bdg) — ISBN 978-0-06-291086-8 (trade bdg)

Typography by Martha Maynard
22 23 24 25 26   PC/LSCH   10 9 8 7 6 5 4 3 2 1
❖
First Edition

Contents

Surprise!

My name is A.J. and I know what you're thinking. You're thinking about ants. I know, because that's what I'm thinking about.

Did you know that a drone ant lives just three days? *Three days!* That's its whole life! What can you do in three days? That's not even enough time go on a vacation.

Not that drone ants take vacations. Where would they go? Next door? Some vacation!

I looked this up—male mosquitoes only live about one week. That's it.

If you were a male mosquito, I guess you could at least go on a vacation for a week. But as soon as you got home from vacation, you'd drop dead. Bummer in the summer! If I was a mosquito on vacation, I wouldn't be able to enjoy myself because the whole time I'd be thinking about dropping dead the minute I got home. That would be one crummy vacation.

My parents are forty-something years

old. That's *really* old. Well, it's old compared to ants and mosquitoes, anyway. I'd rather be a person than an ant or a mosquito. At least you can take a vacation without worrying so much.

The point is, I was in Mr. Cooper's class at school the other day. We had just pledged the allegiance and did Word of the Day.

"Turn to page twenty-three in your math books," said Mr. Cooper.

Ugh. I hate math. When I grow up, I'm going to be a professional skateboarder. I won't need to know math. I'll need to know how to do a kickflip. Why don't they teach *that* in school?

But it must have been my lucky day. Before I could open my math book, an announcement came over the loudspeaker.

"Grades K through five, please report to the all-porpoise room for a surprise assembly."

YAY! (That's also YAY backward.) Surprises are cool.

Well, not *all* surprises. If I was walking down the street and a zombie jumped out from behind a tree and ate my brains, that would be a surprise. But it wouldn't be very cool.

"Pringle up, everybody," Mr. Cooper said.

We got in line and walked a million hundred miles to the all-porpoise room.* The whole school was in there. I had to sit between crybaby Emily and annoying Andrea, this girl with curly brown hair.

"I'll be back in a few minutes," Mr. Cooper told us.

He got up and went backstage behind the curtain. I noticed that a bunch of other teachers got out of their seats and

*I don't know why they call it the all-porpoise room. There are no dolphins in there.

went backstage too.

Hmmm, that was weird.

"I bet the teachers are going to put on a play for us," said Andrea, clapping her hands.

"I'm sure you're right," said Emily, who always thinks Andrea is right.

But the teachers didn't put on a play for us. Instead, the weirdest thing in the history of the world happened. Mr. Klutz, our principal, walked into the all-porpoise room.

Well, that's not the weird part. Mr. Klutz walks into the all-porpoise room all the time. The weird part was what happened next.

All the teachers jumped out from behind the curtain and yelled, "SURPRISE!" A big banner dropped down from the ceiling . . . HAPPY 65th BIRTHDAY, MR. KLUTZ!

WOW! (That's MOM upside down.) I didn't know Mr. Klutz was sixty-five years

HAPPY 65TH BIRTHDAY, MR. KLUTZ!

old. That's almost a *hundred*.

Ms. Hall, our lunch lady, wheeled out a big cake, with lots of candles on it. Everybody sang "Happy Birthday." Mr. Klutz made a wish and blew out the candles.

"Are we getting cake?" I whispered to Andrea.

"Is that all you care about, Arlo?" she whispered back. "Cake?"

"No," I told her. "I also care about cookies and ice cream and candy."

Andrea rolled her eyes. Why can't a truck full of cake fall on Andrea's head? I was going to say something mean to her, but you'll never believe who walked into the door at that moment.

Nobody! It would hurt if you walked

into a door. Doors are made of wood. But you'll never believe who walked into the door*way*.

It was Dr. Carbles, the president of the Board of Education! He's a mean man who drives a tank, and he's always trying to shut down our school. What is his problem?

Dr. Carbles was all smiles as he climbed up on the stage and put his arm around Mr. Klutz. That was weird. Everybody started whispering.

"I thought Dr. Carbles hated Mr. Klutz," whispered Andrea.

"Me too," whispered Emily, who always thinks everything Andrea thinks.

"Dr. Carbles!" said Mr. Klutz. "To what

do we owe the pleasure of your company?"

That's grown-up talk for "What are *you* doing here?"

"I have an announcement to make," said Dr. Carbles.

"Dr. Carbles has an announcement to make!" whispered Michael, who never ties his shoes.

"Dr. Carbles has an accountant to make!" whispered Alexia, this girl who rides a skateboard all the time.

"Dr. Carbles has a mountain to rake!" whispered Neil, who we call the nude kid even though he wears clothes.

"Dr. Carbles has a muffin to bake!" whispered Ryan, who will eat anything, even stuff that isn't food.

"Dr. Carbles is going to jump in a lake!" whispered Emily.

Everybody was buzzing. But not like bees. That would be weird.

"I wanted to wish you a happy sixty-fifth birthday, Mr. Klutz," said Dr. Carbles, "and to congratulate you on your retirement."

WHAT?!

Mr. Klutz was retiring? He never told us that. He looked as surprised as we were. All the teachers just stood there with their mouths open. Everybody was in shock.

There was only one person on the stage who had a smile on her face. It was our vice principal, Mrs. Jafee.

"According to Board of Education rule number 456789," said Dr. Carbles, "sixty-five years old is the mandatory retirement age for principals *blah blah blah blah . . .*"

He went on like that for a while.

"Uh . . . I've never heard of rule number 456789," said Mr. Klutz.

"Yeah, I just wrote it yesterday," said Dr. Carbles.

A big banner dropped down from the ceiling and covered up the first banner . . .

HAPPY RETIREMENT, MR. KLUTZ!

Suddenly, everybody started yelling and screaming and hooting and hollering and freaking out.

"NOOOOOOOO!" shouted Michael.

"Say it ain't so!" shouted Alexia.

"We love Mr. Klutz!" shouted Neil.

13

"Don't go!" shouted Ryan.

Some of the first graders were crying.

Even some of the *teachers* were crying.

This was the worst thing to happen since National Poetry Month.

"We wouldn't have thrown you a surprise party," said Mr. Cooper, "if we had known *this* was going to happen."

Mr. Klutz held up his hand and made a peace sign, which means shut up. He took the microphone off its stand.

"It's okay," he told us. "Calm down, everyone. All things must pass. Maybe it's for the better. I was going to retire in a few years anyway *blah blah blah blah . . .*"

Dr. Carbles grabbed the microphone out of Mr. Klutz's hand.

"Okay, beat it, you rotten kids!" he shouted. "Go back to your classes and learn something for a change!"

We pringled up and walked back to our classroom. As we were passing by the principal's office, I saw Mr. Klutz taking his name plate off the door with a screwdriver.

"Hey Klutz!" shouted Dr. Carbles. "You have five minutes to clear out your office. And don't let me see you back here, ever!"

Dr. Carbles was rubbing his hands together and saying "Bwa-ha-ha," which is what grown-ups always do when they plan to take over the world.

"At last, I got rid of that loser Klutz," muttered Dr. Carbles. "With him out of the way, I can hire a *new* principal. A principal who is totally incompetent. Then I can shut down this terrible school."

Okay, I have two questions: Why was Dr. Carbles talking to himself? And why would he want a principal who can't go to the bathroom?

That didn't make any sense at all.

Dr. Carbles is losing his marbles.

The Long Goodbye

Everybody was sad that Mr. Klutz had to retire. It was hard to pay attention in Mr. Cooper's class while he was trying to teach us math and social studies.

"Okay, everyone," said Mr. Cooper. "Let's try to focus."

"Why should we try to focus?" I asked.

"We're not cameras."

"Not *that* kind of focus, Arlo!" said Andrea, who calls me by my real name because she knows I don't like it.

I was just yanking Andrea's chain. I know what focus means.

When it was time for lunch, none of us were in the mood to eat. We went out to play on the monkey bars during recess, but all anybody could talk about was Mr. Klutz.

"I can't believe he has to retire," Ryan said with tears in his eyes.

"Mr. Klutz is the only principal we've ever had."

"And he's not even that old," said Alexia.

"Bald men don't look as old as they are," said Neil, "because they can't lose any more hair."

"I heard that when some people get old," I said, "they get put on ice floes and floated off into the sunset."

"That's not a thing, Arlo," Andrea said, rolling her eyes.

"It is too a thing," I told her.

"No way that's a thing," said Andrea.

"It's a thing!" I insisted.

We went back and forth like that for a while.

"Oooh, A.J. and Andrea are arguing about what a thing is," said Ryan. "They must be in *love*!"

"When are you gonna get married?" asked Michael.

If those guys weren't my best friends, I would hate them.

Andrea and I kept arguing over whether or not it was a thing to put old people on ice floes. Then I remembered that we were talking about Mr. Klutz. He was a great principal.

"One time," I said, "I got sent to the principal's office because I was bad. I thought Mr. Klutz was going to punish me, but instead he gave me a candy bar."

"Remember the time he climbed up to the top of the flagpole and got stuck there?" asked Ryan.

"Remember the time he let us dye his head like an Easter egg?" asked Alexia.

"Remember the time he married a turkey?" asked Michael.

Ah, those were the good old days. Mr. Klutz was nuts, but he was a good principal.

"I bet we're going to get some boring, *normal* principal," said Neil.

"Maybe Mrs. Jafee will be our new principal," said Emily.

"Yes," agreed Andrea. "When the president leaves office in the middle of

22

the term, the vice president becomes president. So Mrs. Jafee should be the new principal."

"Mrs. Jafee is no fun at all," groaned Michael.

That's when the weirdest thing in the history of the world happened. A marching band marched out of the school. They formed a line on the playground and started to play some song called "Hail to the Chief."*

"Where did that marching band come from?" asked Ryan.

"Rent-A-Marching-Band," I told him. "You can rent anything."

---

*That was weird. It wasn't even raining.

Our custodian, Miss Lazar, rolled a long red carpet out onto the playground. Mr. Klutz came out of the school and walked on the red carpet. Some soldiers came out and gave a twenty-one-gun salute. Five jet planes flew in formation overhead.

I didn't realize that changing principals was such a big deal!

Suddenly, there was a weird sound in the distance. I couldn't tell what it was at first.

"Look, up in the sky!" shouted Andrea. "It's a bird!"

"No, it's a plane!" shouted Ryan.

Actually, it was a helicopter. It was blue, and it hovered over our heads and landed on the blacktop. Miss Lazar set up a microphone for Mr. Klutz. We gave him a round of applause.

"Thank you, students," he said. "It has been my honor *blah blah blah blah* all these years at Ella Mentry School *blah blah blah blah* fine young people *blah blah blah blah* carry on *blah blah blah blah* youth of America *blah blah blah blah* future lies in your hands *blah blah blah blah* . . ."

He said some more stuff, but I was looking at the helicopter. Helicopters are cool.

Mr. Klutz climbed into the helicopter as we all waved goodbye. There was a lot of sniveling and sobbing and slobbering.

Some of the teachers blew their noses into tissues.

Well, not exactly. They just blew their *snot* into the tissues. It would be weird to blow your *nose* into a tissue. How would you get your nose back on your face?

The helicopter flew away. Mr. Klutz waved goodbye through the little window. It was the end of an era at Ella Mentry School.

"Well, I guess he's gone forever," said Alexia.

"Wait a minute," said Ryan. "Doesn't Mr. Klutz live right down the street? Why is he taking a helicopter? He could walk home."

"It's more dramatic this way," said Andrea.

"I wonder if Mr. Klutz takes a helicopter to the supermarket to do his grocery shopping," I said.

"How did he get a helicopter, anyway?" asked Neil.

"From Rent-A-Helicopter," I told him. "You can rent anything."

Mrs. Jafee, the vice principal, came over to us.

"Okay, everybody," she said. "The show is over. Time to go back to your class."

"Are you going to be the new principal, Mrs. Jafee?" asked Emily.

"Not yet," she said. "Dr. Carbles has

the final decision. Hiring a new principal could take time. He will probably place an ad in the newspaper and interview a bunch of people for the job. It could be weeks or even months before there's a replacement for Mr. Klutz."

"I hope he picks you," said Andrea. "You would make a *great* principal."

"I agree," said Emily, of course.

What a pair of brownnosers those two are. Mrs. Jafee wasn't even the principal yet and they were already sucking up to her.

"It has always been my dream to be a principal," said Mrs. Jafee.

That's when the weirdest thing in the

history of the world happened.

But I'm not going to tell you what it was.

Okay, okay, I'll tell you. But you have to read the next chapter. So nah-nah-nah boo-boo on you!

Meet Mrs. Stoker

Only a few minutes had passed after Mr. Klutz's helicopter flew away. We were about to go back inside the school. But Dr. Carbles came out and told us to stay on the playground. That's when I heard a weird noise up in the sky.

It was *another* helicopter! This one

was red. And it was heading right for the playground!

"It must be our new principal!" somebody shouted.

"I thought *I* would be the new principal!" said Mrs. Jafee.

"Beat it, Jafee," said Dr. Carbles. "Go count the spoons in the lunchroom, or whatever it is vice principals do all day."

"Oh, snap!" said Ryan.

Mrs. Jafee stormed inside the school. She looked really mad.

The helicopter hovered overhead for a few seconds, and then it landed on the blacktop. The rotors stopped spinning. The marching band played that song about hail again. We waited for the helicopter door to open. There was electricity in the air!

Well, not really. If there was electricity in the air, we would have all been electrocuted.

But we were all glued to our seats.

Well, not exactly. We weren't even sitting down. Why would you glue yourself to a seat, anyway? How would you get the glue off your pants?

Dr. Carbles went over to the helicopter and opened the door. A lady stepped out. She was young and skinny, and she had strawberry blonde hair.

"I'd like to introduce the new principal

of Ella Mentry School," announced Dr. Carbles. "This is . . . Mrs. Stoker!"

We all clapped even though she didn't do anything except step out of the helicopter. What's up with that? Getting out of a helicopter isn't any big deal.

"It's great to be here," Mrs. Stoker said into the microphone. "Me, I didn't like school very much when I was a kid. I always got punished for things I didn't do. Like my homework!"

Everybody laughed. Mrs. Stoker smiled.

"No, I wasn't a very good student," she continued. "One time, my teacher asked me to write a sentence with the word 'lettuce' in it. I wrote 'Lettuce out of school early.'"

Everybody laughed again.

"Hey, the new principal is funny!" somebody shouted.

"Yes," she continued, "school was really hard for me. In fact, I almost drowned when I got my report card one time. It's

true. My grades were below C level. Get it? Drowned? Below C level?"

I didn't get it. Only a few kids laughed.

Mrs. Stoker tapped the microphone with her finger.

"Is this thing on?" she asked. "Hey, nice monkey bars over there. I didn't know monkeys were allowed in bars. But seriously, kids, do you know why the kindergartner crossed the playground? To get to the other slide!"

"Ha ha ha!" laughed Dr. Carbles. "You are hilarious, Mrs. Stoker. Welcome to Ella Mentry School."

She told a few more jokes, and then we gave her another round of applause.

As Mrs. Stoker was walking into the school, Andrea ran over to her. Of *course*. It figured that Andrea would try to get in good with the new principal before anybody else.

"My name is Andrea," said Andrea. "Where did you work as a principal before, Mrs. Stoker?"

"Oh, no," replied Mrs. Stoker. "I've never been a principal before."

"So I guess you used to be a teacher?" asked Andrea.

"Nope," said Mrs. Stoker. "I've never been a teacher."

"A librarian?"

"Never."

"Did you work at the Board of Education with Dr. Carbles?"*

"No."

"You must have *some* experience in education," said Andrea. "What did you do before this?"

"Oh, I'm a comedian," Mrs. Stoker replied. "At night, I do stand-up comedy."

What?!

"Yes, I'll be appearing at Giggles Comedy Club all week," said Mrs. Stoker. "That's where I met Dr. Carbles. He was sitting in the front row last night and he asked me if I'd be interested in taking a day job as a school principal. So here I am."

WHAT?! Mrs. Stoker is a joker!

---

*I'm bored of education.

38

Bad Jokes and Dad Jokes

We were told there was going to be another assembly so Mrs. Stoker could introduce herself to everyone from kindergarten to fifth grade. So we walked a million hundred miles to the all-porpoise room again. This time, I got to sit next to Ryan. Mrs. Stoker was up on the stage, waving to everybody as we came in.

"Hey," she said after all the classes were seated. "How is everybody feeling today? Anybody here from out of town?"

"I live here," some first grader shouted.

"Well, it's great to be here," said Mrs. Stoker. "Here is way better than *there*. I'm so excited to be your new principal. I was telling some of the kids out on the playground that I was bad student as a child. *Really* bad."

"How bad were you?" somebody yelled.

"I was so bad," said Mrs. Stoker, "that on the first day of ninth grade I

40

brought a ladder with me."

"Why?" somebody yelled.

"Well, they told me it was *high* school," said Mrs. Stoker. "Get it? Ladder? *High* school?"

A few kids laughed.

"When I was a kid, I used to eat my homework for dessert," continued Mrs. Stoker. "Well, it wasn't my fault. My teacher said our homework was a piece of cake. Ha ha! In my school days, they made us take our tests in the jungle. You know why? Because there were too many cheetahs! Get it?"

Mrs. Stoker doubled over laughing at her own jokes. I made sure to laugh even though they weren't that funny. You should always laugh at the principal's jokes, even if they're not funny. That's the first rule of being a kid.

She went on . . .

"There are so many different kinds of schools, am I right? Surfers go to boarding school. People who sell ice cream go to sundae school."

Boy, she sure knows a lot of jokes.

"Do you know what a witch's favorite school subject is?" continued Mrs. Stoker. "Spelling! Get it? But seriously, did you ever notice that math books seem so sad? Well, they do have a lot of problems."

And she went on . . .

"Do you know what the king of all school supplies is?"

"What?" we shouted.

"The ruler!" said Mrs. Stoker. "Get it? Hey, what's the difference between a teacher and a train?"

"What?" we all shouted.

"A teacher tells you to spit out your gum, but a train goes 'Chew chew'!"

Mrs. Stoker doubled over laughing at her own joke again.

"She is hilarious!" Ryan said to me.

"She's going to be a great principal," I agreed.

Everybody gave Mrs. Stoker a round of applause.

"Well, that's my time, kids," she said. "I'll be here until June. You've been a wonderful audi—"

Mrs. Stoker didn't have the chance to finish her sentence because our vice principal, Mrs. Jafee, stood up and raised her hand.

"May I ask a question?" she said.

"Certainly," said Mrs. Stoker. "Ask away."

"What qualifies *you* to be a principal?" asked Mrs. Jafee.

"OOOOOOOO!" everybody ooooooooed.

"How hard could it be?" Mrs. Stoker replied. "All the principal needs to do is yell at kids and decide whether to have recess inside or outside. I can handle that."

Mrs. Jafee didn't look happy with that answer.

"Excuse me," she said. "Where did you go to college, Mrs. Stoker?"

"I went to the American Comedy Institute," she replied. "I got a B.A. That stands for Basically Amusing."

Mrs. Jafee looked like she was getting madder.

"You must have *some* thoughts about education," she said.

45

"Oh yes," replied Mrs. Stoker. "I'm in favor of it."

Our science teacher, Mr. Docker, put his hand up.

"At Ella Mentry School," he said, "we're very serious about recycling, the environment, and protecting animals. Mrs. Stoker, where do you stand on endangered species?"

"Well, if they're endangered," she said, "I wouldn't stand on them!" Then she doubled over laughing again. "Hey, that's a good one! I think I'll put it in my act."

Some of the teachers looked angry, but Mrs. Stoker didn't seem to notice.

"Oh, before I go," she said, "I have some

good news. We will only have half a day of school tomorrow morning."

"YAY!" we all shouted.

"And we'll have the other half tomorrow afternoon," she continued.

"BOO!" we all shouted, even though I think she was just joking.

Mrs. Stoker said we could go back to our classrooms. As we pringled up and filed out of the all-porpoise room, we passed by Dr. Carbles in the back. He was talking on his cell phone.

"Yes!" he said excitedly. "Mrs. Stoker is even worse

than I thought she would be! The teachers already hate her. All she does is tell dumb jokes. She makes Klutz look like Principal of the Year. This is going to be great! Soon, I'll be able to shut this place down and achieve my lifelong dream . . . turning Ella Mentry School into a toxic waste dump. Bwa-ha-ha!"*

---

*That guy is just mean.

D.E.A.R.

When we got back to Mr. Cooper's class, it was D.E.A.R. time. That stands for DROP EVERYTHING AND READ. We have to sit quietly and read a book for fifteen whole minutes.

Ugh. Reading books is boring. I don't

49

even know why you're reading this one.

I looked around. Ryan was reading. Michael was reading. Alexia was reading. Even Neil was reading, and he hates reading as much as I do. Everybody was reading.

But you know who *wasn't* reading? The biggest reader of them all—Little Miss Perfect! Andrea was sitting there with her mean face on.

"What's the matter?" I whispered to her. "Was your clog-dancing lesson canceled today?"*

"No," Andrea whispered back. "I have a problem with Mrs. Stoker."

"More reading, less talking!" said Mr.

---

*That's a kind of dance that plumbers do.

Cooper. "This is D.E.A.R. time, kids."

"What do you have against Mrs. Stoker?" I whispered to Andrea.

"She's going to make a terrible principal," whispered Andrea.

"But she's funny," I whispered back.

"Stop talking, you two," warned Mr. Cooper.

"Mrs. Stoker is so immature," Andrea whispered. "Grown-ups are supposed to act . . . grown up."

"You need to get a sense of humor transplant," I whispered to Andrea.

"Oooh," whispered Ryan. "A.J. and Andrea are whispering secret messages to each other. They must be in *love*!"

"When are you gonna get married?" whispered Michael.

"I said STOP it!" shouted Mr. Cooper.

"You're going to get us in trouble, Arlo," whispered Andrea.

"Your *face* is in trouble!" I whispered back at her.

"All right," shouted Mr. Cooper. "That's the last straw!"

Huh? What do straws have to do with anything? Why are grown-ups always running out of straws? If you ask me, they should buy a new box of straws before the old one is empty.

"A.J. AND ANDREA!" shouted Mr. Cooper. "BOTH OF YOU. GO TO THE PRINCIPAL'S

OFFICE!"

"What did I do?" I asked.

"But . . . but . . . but . . ."

I giggled because Andrea said "but," which sounds just like "butt" even though it only has one *T*.

Andrea and I walked a million hundred miles to the principal's office. She was so mad she wouldn't speak to me the whole time. Andrea *never* gets in trouble. She probably fig- ured this was going to be on her per- manent record and prevent her from getting into Harvard someday.

When we got to the principal's office, nobody was there. The door was open, so we walked in. The office was almost empty. There was no desk or anything— just a bare brick wall with a stool in front of it and a microphone on a stand. That was weird.

Mrs. Patty, the school secretary, came in. She had two folding chairs.

"Have a seat," she told us. "Mrs. Stoker will be here in a minute. Would you kids like some milk?"

"Uh, okay," Andrea and I replied.

Mrs. Patty went out and came back with

two cartons of milk for each of us.

"Here, have a second carton," she said as she handed us the milk.

"I don't want another carton of milk," I told her.

"You *have* to take another carton," she replied.

"Why?"

"We have a two-drink minimum," said Mrs. Patty.

That was weird.

Andrea and I sat down. The lights went off. Mrs. Patty went over to the micro-phone.

"And now . . ." she said dramatically, "straight from Giggles Comedy Club . . .

put your hands together for our very own . . . Mrs. Stoker!"

A spotlight came on and Mrs. Stoker jogged into the office. Andrea and I clapped.

"Thank you!" Mrs. Stoker said. "It's great to be here. Hey, what are you doing under there?"

"Under where?" I asked.

"Ha ha!" said Mrs. Stoker. "I made you say underwear!"

Andrea rolled her eyes.

"Are you going to punish us for talking during D.E.A.R. time?" she asked.

"Yes," said Mrs. Stoker. "Your punishment is that you have to listen to my

new comedy routine. Did you hear about the embarrassed toilet? It was flushed. That reminds me of the policeman who flushed his toilet. Well, he *had* to. It was his doody!"

Wow, I'd never heard a grown-up say "doody" before. They always say it's okay to say "duty" but we shouldn't say "doody." Nobody knows why. Those words sound way too much alike, if you ask me.

Andrea looked mad.

"Not into toilet humor, eh?" asked Mrs. Stoker. "How about animals, Andrea? Do you like animals?"

"I guess," Andrea replied.

"When I was a little girl, I had a pony,"

said Mrs. Stoker. "He was terrible at singing. Well, he was a little hoarse. Get it? A little horse? And my dog is a terrible dancer. He has two left feet . . . and two right feet."

Andrea rolled her eyes again.

"Why did the dinosaur cross the road?" Mrs. Stoker asked.

"I give up," I said.

"Because chickens didn't exist back then!" she said, doubling over with laughter. "Hey, what did the banana say to the dog?"

"I have no idea," I replied.

"Nothing," said Mrs. Stoker. "Bananas can't talk!"

Andrea rolled her eyes again.

"Can we go back to class now?" she asked. "I promise we won't talk during D.E.A.R. time anymore."

"Not yet," said Mrs. Stoker. "I have a few more animal jokes. Did I tell you about my pet bee? His hair is getting too long. I think I'll give him a buzz cut. Get it? Hey, do you know what's black and white and looks like a penguin?"

"What?" Andrea asked.

"A penguin!" shouted Mrs. Stoker.

"No more!" begged Andrea. "Please! Just give us detention. We'll do *anything*. We'll never talk during D.E.A.R. time again."

"You promise?" asked Mrs. Stoker.

"We promise," Andrea and I said.

"Well, okay," said Mrs. Stoker. "You've been a wonderful audience. Don't forget to tip your waitress, Mrs. Patty, on your way out."

Even I was beginning to have my doubts about Mrs. Stoker. She's ridorkulous!

But Seriously

6

We were in the vomitorium eating lunch. I had a sandwich. Michael had a sandwich. Alexia had a sandwich. Everybody had a sandwich except for Ryan. He had a wich-sand. That's a sandwich with the meat on the outside. Ryan is weird.

"So did Mrs. Stoker give you detention?" asked Neil.

"No," Andrea and I replied.

"Is she going to tell your parents you were talking during D.E.A.R. time?" asked Emily.

"No," I said. "She just made us listen to a million hundred bad jokes."

I looked up. Mrs. Stoker was talking to some fifth graders at the other end of the vomitorium.

"Oh no," said Andrea. "Here she comes. She's going to tell more jokes."

Mrs. Stoker was walking toward our table.

"Hide your face," I said. "Maybe she won't notice us."

We all looked at the ground. If you don't want a grown-up to talk to you, look at the ground. That's the first rule of being a kid.

"It's too late," whispered Andrea. "She sees us."

Mrs. Stoker stopped right in front of our table.

"Hi boys and girls!" she said cheerfully. "Hey, did you ever notice that lunch ladies wear those funny hairnets? What's up with that?"

"Hello, Mrs. Stoker," we all said.

"You know," she told us, "the clock in this lunchroom is slow. Yeah, it's always going back for seconds. Get it? Going back for seconds? Actually, I'm kind of mad at that clock. It really gets me ticked off."

I tried my best to laugh at her jokes, but it wasn't easy.

"But seriously," said Mrs. Stoker. "I opened my refrigerator door the other day and a carrot was blushing."

"Don't ask why the carrot was blushing,"

I whispered under my breath.

"Why was the carrot blushing?" asked Emily.

"It saw the salad dressing!" said Mrs. Stoker. "Get it? Speaking of salad, did you hear about the lettuce that won a race? Yeah, it was a head the whole time."

There was no stopping her. She just kept telling joke after joke.

"My cookie had to go to the hospital," Mrs. Stoker told us. "Yeah, it felt crummy. And my baby strawberries are always crying. Well, their parents were in a jam. And my teddy bear never likes to eat dessert. He says he's stuffed. Hey, what did one plate say to the other plate?

Dinner is on me! Get it?"

Wow, Mrs. Stoker sure knows a lot of food jokes. I looked at Michael. Michael looked at Ryan. Ryan looked at Neil. Neil looked at Alexia. Alexia looked at me. We were all looking at each other.

"Uh, I think it's time for us to go to recess," Alexia said.

"Yeah," we all agreed, picking up our trays.

"Is it recess already?" asked Mrs. Stoker. "Hey, why do they call it recess? Is that when you cess again? What's a cess? I say the best candy to eat after lunch is Recess Pieces. Get it?"

We were going to clear off our plates

and run out of there before she could tell any more jokes, but that's when the weirdest thing in the history of the world happened. Mrs. Jafee came into the vomitorium. She walked right up and stuck her face a few inches from Mrs. Stoker's face. She looked mad.

"We need to talk," said Mrs. Jafee.

"Is there a problem?" asked Mrs. Stoker.

"Yeah," Mrs. Jafee replied. "When Mr. Klutz retired, *I* should have been named the new principal. You are totally unqualified. I have more experience than you. I'm smarter than you. And one more thing . . . I'm *funnier* than you."

"OOOOOOOO!" everybody ooooooooed.

"Oh, snap!" said Ryan.

A hush fell over the vomitorium.

"How *dare* you!" said Mrs. Stoker. "You take that back!"

"No," said Mrs. Jafee. "This school ain't big enough for the both of us."*

Mrs. Jafee and Mrs. Stoker were almost

---

*If your teacher says "ain't ain't a word," tell her to look it up in the dictionary. And then say, "Nah-nah-nah boo-boo on you!"

nose to nose.

"Are you challenging me," asked Mrs. Stoker, "to a . . . joke-off?"

"That's right," said Mrs. Jafee. "Meet me on the playground. After school."

"OOOOOOOO!" everybody ooooooooed.

"I'll *be* there!" said Mrs. Stoker.

The Big Joke-Off

I'd never heard of a joke-off. I didn't know what it was. But the news about the big joke-off between Mrs. Stoker and Mrs. Jafee spread around the school like wildfire.

Well, not exactly. That would have been

dangerous. But when the dismissal bell rang, just about everybody who wasn't taking the bus home went out to the playground. We were all buzzing, which was weird because we're not bees.

Five minutes later, Mrs. Stoker came out of the school and walked over to the middle of the blacktop. Then Mrs. Jafee came out. She was holding a book called *1001 Insults for All Occasions*. They both looked really serious.

"Mrs. Stoker is gonna *crush* Mrs. Jafee," I heard some fourth grader say. "She's a professional comedian."

"You can do it, Mrs. Jafee!" shouted some other kid.

We formed a big circle around Mrs.

Jafee and Mrs. Stoker. Everybody stopped talking.

"I am the rightful principal of Ella Mentry School," said Mrs. Jafee.

"In your dreams!" said Mrs. Stoker. "I was hired fair and square. I got the job. Why don't you go count the spoons in the lunchroom?"*

"OOOOOOOO!" everybody ooooooooed.

"There's only one way to settle this," said Mrs. Jafee. "A joke-off. You and me. No jokes barred. The first one to laugh is the loser. The other one gets to be principal. Agreed?"

"Agreed," said Mrs. Stoker.

---

*Spoons are much funnier than knives and forks, if you ask me.

I guess joke-offs are one of those things that grown-ups do when kids aren't around. Because Mrs. Jafee and Mrs. Stoker seemed to know exactly what to do. They shook hands. Then they stood back-to-back. Then they walked five paces away from each other and turned around.

You should have been there. There was electricity in the air!

Well, not really. We already discussed that in Chapter Three.

Mrs. Jafee went first. She opened her book.

"If you were any dumber," she said to Mrs. Stoker, "somebody would have to water you twice a week."

"OOOOOOOO!" everybody oooooooooed.

"Oh, snap!" said Ryan.

Mrs. Stoker didn't crack a smile.

"That was *totally* pathetic," she said. "I would say you're as dumb as a rock, but at least a rock can hold a door open."

"OOOOOOOO!" everybody oooooooooed.

"Oh, snap!" said Ryan.

Mrs. Jafee didn't laugh. She was frantically flipping through the pages in her book.

"Nice try," Mrs. Jafee said. "Y'know, I thought of you today. It reminded me to take out the garbage."

"OOOOOOOO!" everybody oooooooooed.

"Oh, snap!" said Ryan.

"I fail to see the humor," said Mrs. Stoker. "You're the reason why they have to put directions on shampoo bottles. And by the way, your face makes onions cry."

"OOOOOOOO!" everybody ooooooooed.

"Oh, snap!" said Ryan.

"That's pretty funny," said Mrs. Jafee. "But not funny *enough*. You are more disappointing than an unsalted pretzel. Your teeth are so bad, you can eat apples through a fence. Someday you'll go far, and I hope you stay there. The last time I saw something like you, I flushed it."

"OOOOOOOO!" everybody ooooooooed.

"Oh, snap!" said Ryan.

For a second, it looked like Mrs. Stoker

was about to laugh. But she just sneered at Mrs. Jafee.

"Is that the best you've got?" she said. "It's pathetic. You remind me of a Slinky."

"Why do I remind you of a Slinky?" asked Mrs. Jafee.

"You serve no purpose," said Mrs. Stoker, "and everybody smiles when you get pushed down the stairs."*

"OOOOOOOO!" everybody oooooooooed.

"Oh, snap!" said Ryan.

For a second, Mrs. Jafee didn't react. Maybe she didn't know what a Slinky was. Then the corners of her mouth turned up a little. There was a twinkle in her eye. She

---

*Do this with Slinkys, not people!

looked like she was trying not to laugh.

And then she cracked up.

"Ha ha ha!" said Mrs. Jafee. "Slinky! That's a good one!"

"Mrs. Stoker is the winner!" somebody shouted as the rest of us clapped and cheered. "She gets to be principal!"

"Ha ha ha!" said Mrs. Jafee, doubled over laughing. "You win the joke-off. You're funnier than me. I admit it."

"Maybe you should quit education," Mrs. Stoker said as she walked back toward the school. "You should become an archaeologist."

HA HA HA HA HA

"Why should I become an archaeologist?" asked Mrs. Jafee.

"Because your career is in ruins!" Mrs. Stoker shouted as she walked inside.

"OOOOOOOO!" everybody ooooooooed.

"Oh, snap!" said Ryan.

This Is Not a Drill

I don't know what happened to Mrs. Jafee after that. She wasn't in school the next morning. I don't know if she's ever coming back.

Other than that, it was a perfectly normal day at Ella Mentry School. And by that I mean the weirdest thing in the history of the world happened.

We were in Mr. Cooper's class. Well, that's not the weird part. We're in Mr. Cooper's class every day. We pledged the allegiance and did Word of the Day.

"Okay, everybody," said Mr. Cooper. "Turn to page twenty-three in your math books."

Ugh. Not *again*! Why do we have to learn math if we have calculators?

That's when the weird stuff started happening. An announcement came over the loudspeaker. It was Mrs. Stoker.

"Good morning, students and teachers," she said. "Hey, did you hear they're going to start putting babies in the army? Yeah, they'll be in the infantry. Get it? Infantry? Babies?"

I didn't get it.

"But seriously," continued Mrs. Stoker, "our security guard, Officer Spence, has an announcement to make."

That was weird. Officer Spence hardly ever makes announcements.

"Starting right now," said Officer Spence, "we are in a lockdown situation. You all know what to do."

A lockdown drill? You know what that means. No math! Yay!

Mr. Cooper slammed his math book closed. He looked *really* mad. Every time he tries to teach page twenty-three in our math books, there's some kind of interruption.*

"We had a lockdown drill *last* week," Mr. Cooper said. "Why do we have to do another one so soon?"

---

*Just in case you didn't notice.

Do they have lockdown drills in your school? That's when you have to lock the whole school down. So it has the perfect name. At our school, we have a lockdown drill every few months. Mr. Klutz always said we had to be prepared for any kind of emergency situation.

We knew what to do. Everybody got out of their seats and moved to the wall in the corner of the classroom, away from the doors and windows.

"I bet some aliens from another planet have landed," whispered Neil.

"It could be zombies," whispered Michael.

"It's probably alien zombies," I whispered.

"I'm scared," whispered Emily, who's scared of everything.

"Shhhhhhh!" said Mr. Cooper. "Quiet, everyone."

"Speaking of drills," said Mrs. Stoker over the loudspeaker, "the other day I drilled some holes in two pieces of metal and bolted them together. At first it was boring, but then it was riveting. Get it? Drills? Boring? Riveting?"

I didn't get it.

"Mrs. Stoker shouldn't be making jokes during a lockdown drill," whispered Andrea. "It's not appropriate."

For once in her life, Little Miss Perfect was right. Lockdowns are serious stuff. We're supposed to stay completely quiet and wait until somebody announces "all clear."

"Did you hear about the guy who got caught drilling a hole in a fence?" Mrs. Stoker continued over the loudspeaker. "The police are looking into it. Hey, do you know why hens are so good at fire drills? They know where to exit. Get it? Exit? Egg sit?"

"KNOCK IT OFF!" Officer Spence

suddenly shouted. "No more jokes! I need all the students and teachers to go to the all-porpoise room *immediately*. This is *not* a drill!"

"What's going on, Officer Spence?" asked Mrs. Stoker.

"We have an intruder!" he shouted at her.

The Big Surprise Ending

9

WHAT?! An intruder? This *was* serious.

We all rushed to line up in single file. Andrea was the line leader. Ryan was the door holder. Mr. Cooper looked worried as we hurried down the hall and walked a million hundred miles to the all-porpoise room. Nobody was talking or making jokes. All the classes from kindergarten to fifth grade filed into the room.

"What's going on?" I heard Mr. Cooper ask Officer Spence.

"I was watching the security cameras," replied Officer Spence, "and I spotted a suspicious-looking person wearing a mask lurking around the playground."

While we took our seats, Officer Spence went over and locked the doors of the all-porpoise room. Then he locked the windows and closed the shades. Finally, he turned off the lights.

It was completely dark in the all-porpoise room. I couldn't see my own hand in front of my face.

"Okay, everyone stay low and stay quiet," said Officer Spence. "Stay away from windows and doors. Teachers, please silence your cell phones."

"I'm scared," whimpered Emily.

For once in her life, Emily had a good reason to be scared. We were all scared.

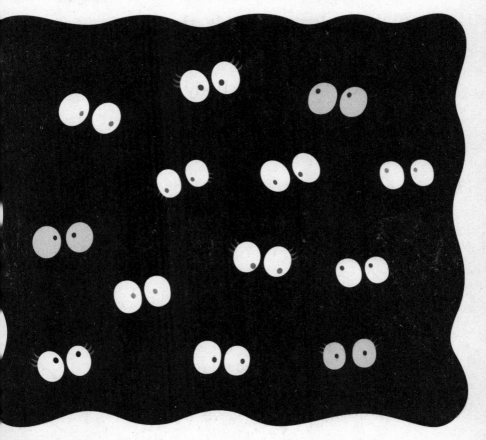

"Everything is going to be all right," said Officer Spence. "Stay calm. I will protect you."

We all got quiet. Mrs. Stoker looked like she might be tempted to crack a joke, but she stopped herself. After a million hundred minutes, I heard some footsteps in the hallway outside the all-porpoise room.

"Who's that?" somebody whispered.

"Shhhhhhhh!"

The footsteps were getting closer.

And closer.

And closer.

And closer.

And closer.

And closer.

And closer.

Okay, we get it.

And closer.

And closer.

And closer.

And closer.

Knock it off already.

And closer.

And closer.

And closer.

And then, there was a knock at the door.

"Don't answer it!" somebody whispered.

There was another knock at the door. A louder knock.

"They're gonna break down the door!"

somebody whispered.

"Speaking of doors," said Mrs. Stoker, "the other day, a policeman knocked on my door and told me my dogs were chasing people on bikes. That's crazy! My dogs don't know how to ride bikes."

"Shhhhh!" shushed Officer Spence.

"Mrs. Stoker should really stop cracking jokes," whispered Andrea. "This is a serious situation."

"Let me in!" somebody shouted from the other side of the door.

Then there was banging on the door.

"Open up!" the person shouted from the other side of the door.

Mrs. Stoker looked like she was going to

crack another joke, but Officer Spence put one finger in front of his lips.

"Shhhh!" he whispered. "Don't make a sound!"

We were all on pins and needles.

Well, not really. That would have hurt. We were just sitting there in the dark.

But it was intense.

Well, not exactly. We weren't in tents. We were sitting on seats.

It sounded like the person on the other side of the door was trying to pick the lock with a screwdriver or something. Officer Spence rushed over to the door.

And then suddenly, the door swung open and somebody burst into the

all-porpoise room! The person was wearing a dark mask, so we couldn't tell who it was.

"Freeze, dirtbag!" shouted Officer Spence.

He pulled the mask off the intruder. And you'll never believe in a million hundred years who it was.*

I'm not gonna tell you.

Okay, okay, I'll tell you.

It was Mr. Klutz!

"GASP!" everybody gasped.

Betcha didn't see *that* coming!

"All clear!" shouted Officer Spence. "Relax, everybody. The lockdown is over."

---

*I can't take the suspense any longer!

We all breathed a sigh of relief. Everybody started buzzing. But not like bees.

"Is Dr. Carbles here?" asked Mr. Klutz, looking all over.

"No," said Officer Spence.

"Good," said Mr. Klutz. "He banned me

from the school."

"Then why are you here?" asked Officer Spence.

"I wanted to see what you would do in an emergency situation without me around," Mr. Klutz replied. "Where's Mrs. Stoker?"

Mrs. Stoker was sort of hiding in the corner near the flag.

Mr. Klutz marched over to her. He looked really serious.

"This isn't funny!" he shouted at her. "The principal of a school has a very important job! She is responsible for the safety of hundreds of children! There is a time for fooling around and a time to be serious. You need to act like a principal!"

WOW! (That's MOM upside down.) I'd never heard a grown-up get yelled at before. Mrs. Stoker looked really upset. Then the weirdest thing in the history of the world happened.

She started crying.

Everybody stopped buzzing and looked at her. It was so quiet you could hear a pin drop.

Well, that is, if anybody brought pins to school with them. But why would anybody do that? Pins are sharp. You could poke out somebody's eye with one of those things.

"You're right, Mr. Klutz," Mrs. Stoker

sobbed, hanging her head. "I'm sorry. I tell way too many jokes. It's a big problem. I just can't seem to stop myself."

She pulled a tissue out of her pocket and blew her nose into it. Well, she didn't *actually* blow her nose into the tissue. But you know what I mean.

"It's okay," Mr. Klutz said as he gave Mrs. Stoker a hug. "Nobody is perfect. We all have our little quirks."

I didn't know what a quirk was, but I made a mental note to get a little one after I got home from school. Everybody gave Mrs. Stoker a round of applause.

"I'm sure you're going to be a great principal," Mr. Klutz told her.

"I'll try to be better in the future," she replied. "And speaking of the future, do you know why the astronauts of the future will be cooking hamburgers on asteroids?"

Oh no.

"I give up," said Mr. Klutz. "Why will the astronauts of the future be cooking hamburgers on asteroids?"

"To make them a little meteor!" Mrs. Stoker replied. "Get it? Meteor? Meatier? Ha ha ha! Too soon? It's okay, I got a million of 'em! Kids, are you with me? I know you're out there. I can hear you breathing . . ."

That's pretty much what happened at school. I got to see it with my own eyes. Well, it would be pretty hard to see something with somebody else's eyes.

Maybe Mrs. Stoker will stop cracking bad jokes all the time. Maybe Mr. Klutz will take a helicopter to do his grocery shopping. Maybe Mr. Cooper will buy a new box of straws. Maybe Mrs. Jafee will count the spoons in the lunchroom. Maybe Dr. Carbles will go jump in a lake. Maybe Andrea's clog-dancing lesson will be canceled.

Maybe they'll put babies in the army. Maybe we'll get the glue out of our pants. Maybe alien zombies will attack the school. Maybe the astronauts of the future will cook hamburgers on asteroids.

But it won't be easy!